THE

VOIVOD

A GHOST STORY

CORAX

DOMINIC SELWOOD

Published in Great Britain by
CORAX
London

Visit our author website and blog
www.dominicselwood.com

ISBN 978-0-9926332-5-7

Cover design and typesetting by Odyssey Books
Set in Baskerville 11/15

ABOUT THE AUTHOR

Dominic Selwood is the Amazon no. 1 bestselling author of the crypto-thriller, *The Sword of Moses*. He is also the author of *Knights of the Cloister*, a history of the medieval Knights Templar and Knights Hospitaller. He writes for the UK's *Daily Telegraph* newspaper, and has appeared as a historical expert on numerous TV and radio programmes. He also acts as a historical consultant for film and industry. He studied at university in Oxford, the Sorbonne, London, Poitiers, and Wales, and has taught and lectured on warfare, religion, heresy, and all the fun stuff. He is an elected Fellow of the Royal Historical Society and an English barrister. He lives in London with his wife and two children, and has never stopped writing and researching.

By the same author

Fiction

THE SWORD OF MOSES

Non-Fiction

KNIGHTS OF THE CLOISTER

For more information, visit
www.dominicselwood.com

TO

ANTHONY WHITEHOUSE
(1922–1992)

WHO FIRST READ TO ME

THE STORIES OF

M R JAMES

Russell Square
London
27 January 1897

NOW THAT I have read the letter from my good friend, Dr Sir Oberon Worsley, F.S.A., F.B.A., M.A., D.PHIL., and have had time to contemplate its dreadful contents, I find myself at my wits' end. Although I struggle adequately to comprehend the events he describes, the correspondence has led me to the point of a nervous terror.

I dare not leave my house, although I perceive there is no safety for me within it either. I despair of how to warn others. Yet I fear that in the account I am now writing may lie the very evil which besets me. Nevertheless, since my hours are now doubtless numbered, I feel no alternative except to commit the abominable matter to paper in the hope that some salvation may yet be found.

Last Wednesday, the 20th, I received by the evening mail a letter from my good friend Worsley, who recently retired as Bodley's Librarian. He had held the post at Oxford with distinction for many years, and in that time did much for the scholars of that great city. He and I had known each other since we were undergraduates at Magdalen in the '50s, and, as I have always maintained my literary interests, we have kept up a regular and cordial correspondence.

The letter arrived as I was dressing for dinner. For the last several years, it has been my habit to dine at home rather than in my Club during the bitter evenings of January, when the chill air does me no good. So I took Worsley's letter with me to the table, where, for reasons which will become apparent, I was keenly anticipating reading it with the roast goose Stephens had earlier procured, along with a bottle of the '65 Haut-Brion that we agreed would suit the dish admirably.

However, the news Worsley recounted in his letter rendered me quite incapable of dining, and an hour later I waved the plate away, untouched, fearing for my reason.

The extraordinary and ghastly tale he recounted was this.

— o O o —

A month or so ago, the senior staff at the Bodleian had thrown a farewell party for Worsley at the Randolph. When the final cigars had been smoked and goodbyes said, he retired to the comfortable house he kept in

Shropshire. There he set about arranging his papers to prepare for the many monographs he looked forward to composing now he had the luxury of time and uninterrupted thought. His primary interests lay in northern European *incunabula*, although a lifetime in the company of all manner of books had brought him familiarity with an exceptionally wide range of printed and manuscript materials, and these were all to be the subject of his scholarship.

However, before he commenced these learned activities, he set about compiling a brief account of his career's most memorable events. This was not for any purpose of vanity, as any who know him will appreciate, but rather a record of what had transpired at that great library during his tenure. Such an account would, he felt, be a useful resource for his successors, as all too often the details of major acquisitions passed with inadequate note kept of the circumstances.

And so he had begun with his early years, adumbrating the circumstances of the larger bequests left to the care of the library, as well as some of the more significant purchases he had made on its behalf.

At this stage of the letter, his tone became more intimate, and he begged me not to think any the less of him for what he was about to relate. I was taken aback by the plea, as I had no reason to suppose my regard for him would diminish, so I read on, unperturbed but curious.

Some years after his appointment, he had been invited by a private connection to an auction in Cracow. The catalogue listed the extensive library of a recently deceased aristocrat of that region, who had spent a lifetime assembling a range of rare and ancient works, especially those related to the history of heresy and pagan religions.

Worsley had thought it a fascinating and unique collection, and was particularly taken with a thirteenth-century codex from the great scriptorium of Lambach Abbey in Austria, which contained, so the catalogue detailed, various writings of the friar and scholar, Roger Bacon, as well as several of his contemporary English Franciscans. Worsley suspected that the manuscript might be out of his price range, but there were also reasonable guide prices for sundry other desirable works, along with numerous library staples that he was sure he could place with some of the university's faculty and college libraries.

In the event, to Worsley's disappointment but not his surprise, the Bacon went to the agent of a private collector from Trondheim, but he was nevertheless able to salvage the trip by acquiring, among other works, an excellent price on Migne's 161-volume *Patrologia Graeca*, dating from before the plates were tragically burned then badly reconstructed. He also managed to procure a well-preserved collection of the works of Isaac Casaubon, which came bundled in a job lot together with a random assortment of miscellaneous and unnoteworthy volumes that Worsley determined to sell on to one of those London dealers specializing in fitting out 'ornamental' libraries by the yard.

However, around a month and a half later, when the heavy wooden crates were duly delivered to his office at the Bodleian, Worsley was startled to find that among the extra books he had been planning to sell was one exceedingly curious item, which he took out and laid on his desk to examine more closely.

It was of the quarto size, bound in a thick but soft brown leather, with large, loose folds extending from the front and back boards, enabling the volume to be fully swathed before being fastened tight with laces. With mounting excitement, Worsley untied it, knowing that this style of binding could suggest a medieval codex or manuscript of considerable age.

As the cover fell away to reveal the contents, Worsley could not stifle a gasp. There, before him, were some seventy folios of the highest quality vellum, still as soft and linen-like as the day they had first been assembled. He turned the leaves one by one, and they disclosed the same Cyrillic orthography throughout, written in a bold, clear hand. The text was not intelligible to Worsley, who did not number the Slavic languages among his considerable linguistic accomplishments, but he could nevertheless immediately determine from the layout of the text that this was not a standard ecclesiastical, exegetical, philosophical, or other instructional work. It frequently devolved into what appeared to be lists, and on most pages there were one or more gaps before the text restarted with a fresh superscription. The condition of the whole was magnificent, apart from some light but frequent foxing which was of little consequence, representing probably no more than a dusting of fungal matter, or the residue of water damage of the sort that regularly disfigured books of a like age.

If Worsley had to guess, he would say the codex was a diary. But he almost dared not hope that might be the case, as all his experience told him that the size, type of vellum, binding, ink, script, and overall impression suggested it dated from the early 1500s, and an unknown diary from that period could be a very valuable volume indeed, not merely as a physical object, but for the information it would inevitably reveal about the owner and his environment.

With no delay, Worsley wrapped the soft codex in a piece of clean white linen, tucked it into his Gladstone bag, then hurried with it across the Old Schools Quad to the Sheldonian, down past the site where heretics had once burned on the Broad, and around the corner to the imposing gateway of St John's. After greeting the porter, he climbed the narrow wooden stairs in the front quadrangle to the rooms of a man he knew could unlock the mysteries of the volume.

Professor Nicolai Dolgorukov's rooms were immaculately neat, and lined with floor-to-ceiling bookcases on which nestled, in addition to his personal library, exotic almond-eyed icons from the Russian Orthodox tradition. Dolgorukov was the university's leading Russian cultural expert, and Worsley felt sure the white-haired scholar would be able to decipher the codex.

Once Worsley had carefully unwrapped the book and laid it onto the round table in the window bay, Dolgorukov began to pore over it, fascinated, muttering as he turned the leaves, examining samples of text from various points within the book.

It did not take Dolgorukov long to reach a verdict, which he offered to Worsley with absolute certainty. The codex was written in Chancery Slavonic, and given the specifics of the style, it unmistakeably originated from the Grand Duchy of Lithuania, sometime around A.D. 1500. More than that Dolgorukov could not say. He was acquainted with Chancery Slavonic of the place and period, but required access to some specialist grammars and lexicons to make sense of the codex. If Worsley would leave it with him for a week or so, he felt sure he would be able to present the librarian with a detailed assessment.

Worsley was delighted, and headed home feeling the excitement of a collector who has, quite accidentally, perhaps stumbled upon a piece of considerable importance.

However, when the week was up, Professor Dolgorukov did not reply, and nor did he make contact for the following three days. Accordingly, the next morning, Worsley resolved to pay a visit to Dolgorukov at St John's in the evening once the library had closed. But, as he turned to the day's correspondence waiting on his desk, he was immediately interrupted by the appearance in his doorway of two university Bulldogs. With regret, they informed him, Professor Dolgorukov was dead, and the city's police wished to speak with Bodley's Librarian.

Shocked, Worsley acquiesced, and the Bulldogs showed in a grim-looking inspector of police, who explained that Professor Dolgorukov's scout had found him lifeless in his rooms that morning. What interested the inspector most for the moment, though, was a pocketbook Dolgorukov had been keeping, in which Worsley's name had been mentioned several times in the last week.

The inspector seated himself, and handed a small soft-backed pocketbook to Worsley along with the assurance that the entries told the story better than he could.

With a sense of foreboding, Worsley took the slim volume and began to read.

— o O o —

Professor Dolgorukov's first spidery notes relating to the codex began with his initial analysis and assessment.

The manuscript was, he stated, the work of Radvila Pac, the Voivod of Trakai, an influential nobleman from the Duchy of Lithuania, whom Dolgorukov noted had lived in the turbulent years between A.D. 1473 and 1536.

The first entry in the codex was dated February 1507 at Trakai Island Castle, Lake Galvė. By laborious researches Dolgorukov had managed to ascertain that the Voivod had, some while earlier, and under unclear circumstances, taken permanent leave of the court in Vilnius, and retired west, to his family estate at Trakai.

As Dolgorukov began his reading of the codex, he at first surmised it to be a record of the Voivod's household accounts, which began with a detailed list of various refurbishments to the great castle on the lake. However, this struck Dolgorukov as odd, and he could not immediately comprehend why keeping such a record would be the preserve of the Voivod himself and not some clerk of works or a functionary with similar responsibilities. However, there could be no doubt. The work was written in the personal hand of the Voivod.

As Dolgorukov progressed further into the codex, he noted the inclusion of more specific entries relating to heavy building works, which he concluded to involve the stabilization of certain existing structures and substantial excavations underneath those sections. The purchase of significant quantities of wood, metal, and stone was accounted for, and a large amount of earth was carted away. All the evidence pointed to the Voivod's engaging in the construction of substantial new castle cellars.

As the works progressed, further notable items appeared in the lists of expenditure. Large quantities of raw iron were ordered, and Dolgorukov noted that eight blacksmiths, together with their apprentices, were retained to work special furnaces built on site to process the metal and fit it into the cellars.

Dolgorukov also noted a reference to the *Hygromanteia*, a book with which he was unfamiliar, but which the Voivod had installed into some manner of oratory he was also having constructed. The inventory noted that the chapel was furnished with censers, lamps, and the usual assortment of bowls and chalices, but there were no references to any of the normal liturgical texts or vestments, or to any payment to the local bishop for the consecration of the chapel. Furthermore, the dimensions of the oratory's great stone font seemed implausible, and Dolgorukov made a note to check whether he really had understood correctly that it was large enough to receive a grown man, as well as the slightly odd, but nevertheless precise, specification that it contain a tap in the pedestal for drawing off liquid from the font's great basin.

At this stage, Dolgorukov broke off to record that he was only able to work on the codex for a few hours that day. He had lain up in bed for much of the morning, exhausted, having awoken in terror in the middle of the night after a harrowing and vivid vision in which some blasphemous force had hounded him into the depths of the chthonic pit, where he became one with the beasts of the netherworld, and from where his shouts and screams rang out unanswered for all eternity.

The following entry in Dolgorukov's notebook was a continuation of his reading of the codex. And it was here that he came to the first of the many lists Worsley had originally observed.

To the professor's surprise, they were groups of names and ages, and a modest analysis of the specifics permitted him to conclude that they were not nobles, but instead common people from the locality. And yet it was not clear to Dolgorukov what involvement these individuals could have had in the castle refurbishments, as many of them were women. The lists were therefore unlikely to be records of accounts paid to workers, and, in any event, no sums of disbursed money were detailed.

Dolgorukov's notes began once more the next day with an admission of his extreme mental exhaustion.

The previous night he had again been visited by terrifying visions in which his fate was intertwined with those of the diabolical legions of the fiery realm. He had felt his immortal soul being drawn irreversibly into their kingdom of damnation, and had struggled wildly, but in vain, to free himself from the weight of their unholy dominion. As a rational man, these Hadean visions had clearly shaken him, for he had found difficulty putting into words his certainty of something malign in his room the previous evening — some force that was orchestrating the nocturnal terrors.

As Dolgorukov progressed further into the codex and analysed ever more of the lists, which seemed to appear every month or so, he observed that the individuals mentioned were invariably youthful — a peculiarity that was not impossible among the local workforce, but which was nevertheless, in Dolgorukov's opinion, improbable. He also noted that, so far, no two names were identical in any of the lists, suggesting that these were not records of a permanent or skilled workforce.

Dolgorukov's next entry was in an altogether more erratic hand. He had retired to bed in his college rooms at around 11.00 P.M. the previous evening, as was his custom. After falling asleep, the unholy nightmares had begun again as he found himself wrapped in the suffocating, pestilential embrace of

Abaddon, the exterminating angel, whose foul and mighty wings of decay were speeding him into the farthest reaches of hell. As the monstrous angel let go and dropped him headlong into the hot, foetid void, he awoke with a shout of abject terror.

But worse was to come, for as he lay awake in the dark, listening to his thundering heart and ragged breathing, he felt a chill of horror at the sound of a faint scratching emanating from the corner of his bedchamber. He tried to reason with himself that it indicated no more than the presence of mice. But as his senses strained in the gloom and he thought he could hear their furry bodies rubbing against each other, he gradually came to realize that he could see a large pair of narrow, glowing, yellow eyes fixed on him from the darkened corner of the chamber.

Seized by a dread fear, he struck a match and re-illuminated his candle, but when the light dispelled the darkness there was nothing untoward visible. However, when he carried the guttering wick over to the spot, he received a mortal shock on beholding what appeared to be faint, but clearly fresh, scratch marks in the floorboards. With his heart pounding against his ribcage, he observed that the three short scratches were grouped together, about an inch and a half in length, as if made by the claws of some wild animal.

Dolgorukov did not put his light out again that night, but stayed awake until dawn, while all manner of delirious thoughts raced through his tormented mind.

The next day, despite his exhaustion, he resumed his analysis of the codex, and read further. For many pages the text merely comprised lists of names, around four or five a month. But then there came an entry of an altogether different nature.

The professor could not bring himself to transcribe the details verbatim. However, the text in the codex was unambiguously clear, and in a trembling hand Dolgorukov had related that at this point in the codex the Voivod gave an account of the conclusions he had been able to draw from his researches to date.

The Voivod referred in detail, and explicitly, to the fate of each of the individuals listed in the codex — to burning, maiming, flaying, freezing, boiling, starving, crushing, gouging, mounting on hooks, suspending in cages. The abominable list of depravities went on: the removal of noses, ears, eyes, and other extremities with heated forceps and blades; abascination, impaling, evisceration, and exsanguination. It was a hideous and hellish list of the fate of the poor innocents in the Voivod's secluded dungeons.

Dolgorukov's writing at this stage became so unsteady that it was apparent he was struggling to make sense of the enormities laid out before him in the codex. But the account continued in its merciless detail, and with minute exactitude, chronicling how long the deranged Voivod was able to keep each of the poor mutilated wretches alive whilst subjecting them to unending sadistic tortures. And all the while, it stated, the font in the devilish chapel was kept filled with the victims' lifeblood, which the Voivod drew off and imbibed in blasphemous ceremonies, offering libations to the infernal powers that animated him.

As Dolgorukov continued through the monstrous text, he realized with a sickening horror that the irregular but frequent brown staining marking the pages of vellum could now clearly be understood as the blood of the hapless victims, still on the hands of the butcher as he recorded his bestial experiments.

As the obscenity of the Voivod's depravity sank in, Dolgorukov was now sure that the nightmares which had been afflicting him were no figment of his imagination. He was not prone to nervous seizures, and had never before suffered from any mental disturbances to his sleep. But now he felt certain that the cause lay somehow in the codex, in whatever hellish forces the Voivod had unleashed in his demonic charnel house.

By the time Dolgorukov had made these monstrous discoveries, it was just past the hour when luncheon was served in college. Yet he no longer had any thought of the routines of ordinary life. His febrile mind was plagued with images of the Voivod's unimaginable savagery, and he made in haste for the railway station. He caught the next train to London, and then took a hansom cab directly to the Russian Embassy's chapel in Welbeck Street, where he procured a large flask of holy water and some freshly blessed Eucharistic *prosphora* bread.

Once back in Oxford, he hurried directly through the ancient dark streets back to college, and made straight for the Senior Common Room, where he obtained two silver bowls. On returning to his rooms, he set them carefully under his bed. Into one he placed the large hunk of consecrated *prosphora* bread, while into the other he decanted the entire flask of holy water, pausing only to sprinkle a small amount onto his bed clothes.

Dolgorukov's final entry that evening, made as he retired to bed, noted merely that he was not sure what the coming night would bring, but that he trusted in the mercies of the all-powerful *Pantocrator*, the Lord of Light, that the forces of righteousness would prevail.

— o O o —

There Professor Dolgorukov's notes ended. When Worsley had finished reading the final entry, he handed the worn pocketbook back to the police inspector with an unsteady hand.

What, the Inspector now wished to know, did Worsley make of such an extraordinary tale?

Worsley gave the inspector a full account of how he had visited Cracow and procured the codex, how he had suspected it to be written in a Slavic tongue, and how he had left it with Professor Dolgorukov in order that the professor might investigate whether it was of any value. More than that he could not add, except that he did know about the volume called the *Hygromanteia*, which the Voivod had installed in his blasphemous chapel. It was, he informed the inspector, a notorious thirteenth-century grimoire, or book of black magic. Although it was not rare, and many copies existed, it was nevertheless infamous for its devilry.

After some further interrogation, the police inspector seemed content with the information he had received, and moved to draw the interview to a close. Yet before he left, Worsley could not refrain from enquiring what, exactly, had happened to Professor Dolgorukov.

The old scholar had been found by his scout that morning, the inspector confided. He had been lying dead in bed, his face and limbs blackened and wasted, as if by fire, with an expression of abject terror distorting what was left of his features. Despite a diligent search by the university Bulldogs and the city constabulary, they had managed to find no explanation for the extraordinary death. There was no evidence of a conflagration, and nothing unusual in the professor's rooms. The doors and windows were sealed. No locks had been broken, and the scout had been able to confirm that, so far as he was aware, nothing had been removed. The only seeming irregularity was that under the professor's bed were found two empty silver bowls from the Senior Common Room, one with a few half-chewed morsels of bread in it, as if the leftovers of some animal's meal, and the other with a small clump of coarse damp black hair resting in several drops of clear water.

Worsley's letter to me then continued in a most personal tone. He had never before told anyone of the Voivod's codex, he confided, and immediately after the obsequies for Professor Dolgorukov had been observed, Worsley had secreted the codex in the deepest and farthest reaches of the vast subterranean book stacks under the Bodleian. He had ensured he was unobserved, and had made no record of the codex in any of the library's catalogues, thereby rendering it, to all intents and purposes, gone.

However, now that so many years had passed, he had felt that there was perhaps little harm in writing an account of the affair for his successor. But to his horror, no sooner had he returned to the matter, than he started to be plagued by demonic nightmares similar to the ones that had afflicted the wretched professor. So intense had the nocturnal terrors become these last few days that he feared desperately for his safety. And, most recently, he vouchsafed that he, too, was convinced there was something in his chamber at night that was not of this world. He was, he feared, under the same morbid malediction as the professor.

Worsley ended his letter to me with a warm affirmation of his friendship, but no suggestion of meeting when next he was in town, which was the usual manner in which his correspondence terminated.

Such was the content of the terrible letter I received from Worsley last week.

— o O o —

Under ordinary circumstances, I would have had Stephens pack my travelling bags before procuring the mail train direct to Shropshire. I would have paid Worsley an immediate visit to see if I could arrange the specialist medical attention he required for nervous exhaustion or whatever mental affliction had caused him to compose such a deranged letter.

But instead I found myself sitting immobile in my chair, paralyzed with incredulity, chilled by a nausea running through me. The reason was plain enough. I had known when I first received the correspondence that this was to be no ordinary letter, as that very morning I had opened *The Times* to find the most sad inclusion of Worsley's obituary.

After a period of wrestling with racing thoughts,

my senses returned, and I undertook a rapid comparison of the dates of his death and of the letter, after which it was a simple enough matter to piece together the chronology. Worsley had died in the night immediately after penning me the lengthy missive. His man, no doubt attending to the many matters consequent on his master's demise, must have delayed for several days before entrusting the letter to the post.

I reread the obituary with care, but, as I had correctly recalled, it gave no cause for Worsley's sudden demise, nor details of any irregularities. Now, however, a week after receiving Worsley's fateful correspondence, I am all too well aware of the reason for his untimely death. It is exactly the same as that which carried off Professor Dolgorukov all those years ago. And it is the same that is now focusing its malign attentions on me. For I, too, am now aware of the Voivod's hideous transgressions, and am accordingly wracked with sleeplessness and infernal nightly visions, counting in terror what I know to be my few remaining hours.

It is plain to me that the codex is unholy and cursed. I cannot account for why Worsley was allowed to live on for several decades after becoming aware of its contents. I can only surmise it was related to the fact that, while he had care of the great library, he protected the codex from destruction. And, from what I know of the Bodleian's almost infinite subterranean book stacks, it is likely the codex will live on there, unharmed and undiscovered, for all time.

To prove to myself that I am not going insane, I have since traced the details of the policeman who brought Professor Dolgorukov's pocketbook to Worsley that day, and in some measure I was relieved to discover that he, too, suffered a fatal seizure within a month of the luckless professor. Therefore I am not mad. But I will surely also be dead soon, as the diabolical dreams are becoming unbearable, and I, too, now feel the presence of something unholy drawing near, hastening my destruction.

I only hope that with this slightly redacted and amended account of the hellish matter I have not committed the same sin against the innocent. I have altered the name of the Voivod in question, and provided a different location for his infernal castle. I pray these small discrepancies will succeed in preventing the same fate from befalling whoever may read this, and that, by the grace of God, one will be found who will find a way to free posterity of this monstrous profanity.

Praise for

THE SWORD OF MOSES

Amazon no. 1 Bestseller

'One of the Top 5 religious thrillers of all time'
BESTTHRILLERS.COM

'Rollercoaster crypto-thriller …
move over Lara Croft!'
Five Stars, Editor's Pick of the Week
DAILY EXPRESS

'A fast-paced Biblical thriller backed by impeccable
research. Fans of The Da Vinci Code will love this!'
**J F PENN, USA TODAY BESTSELLING AUTHOR OF
THE ARKANE SERIES**

'Without doubt one of the best books of 2013'
DREAMING.COM

'Brilliant'
HAMPSHIRE CHRONICLE

'Epic'
CIPHERMYSTERIES.COM